The Football Match

Written by Hannah Fish

Illustrated by Dusan Pavlic

Collins

Who's in this story?

Listen and say

Download the audio at www.collins.co.uk/839659

Zoe was good at everything.
At school, Zoe showed everyone in her class her picture.

The children in Zoe's class played fun games in the playground, but not with Zoe.

I'm very good at basketball.

One day, Zoe saw a poster for the school football team.

"I can run fast," said Zoe. "I can play football, too!"

"Football is a team sport, Zoe," said Yuki. "Can you play in a team?"

"This weekend, we have a match," said the teacher, Ms Gil.

"Who with?" asked Mei.

"Finham School," said Ms Gil.

"They're very good at football!" said Lana.

"Don't worry, we can win," said Zoe
"I can score five goals."

It was Saturday – match day.

Zoe was happy. She wanted to score lots of goals.

Zoe ran with the ball.

"Kick the ball to me, Zoe!" said Mei.

Zoe wanted to score a goal. She ran fast, but then a Finham player took the ball from her.

Finham School won the match!

"You needed to kick the ball to us, Zoe," said Mei.

"You play football in a team, Zoe!" said Lana.

On Sunday, Zoe saw Yuki in the park. Zoe was angry. She thought football was a silly game. She wanted to stop playing football now.

Zoe was angry, but Yuki wanted to help her.

"Don't stop playing football, Zoe," said Yuki. "Do you want me to help you?"

"OK," said Zoe.

The team was angry with Zoe.
They wanted a team player!

Yuki was very nice to Zoe. She showed her how to play football and how to play in a team.

That week, Zoe and Yuki played football in the park every day after school.

Zoe is better at football now.

This weekend, we have the big match," said the teacher. "With a very good team – Hutton School."

"Not with Hutton School!" said Mei.

"They win all their matches!" said Lana.

Oh dear!

It was Saturday – big match day.

Hutton School had one goal. But now Mei had the ball, she ran and kicked it to Lana. Lana saw Zoe and kicked the ball to her.

Zoe ran with the ball. She saw the goal and ran fast.

Zoe saw Yuki and she kicked the ball to her. Yuki ran with the ball, and then she scored a goal!

Both teams scored a goal each! They played very well and everyone was happy.

"Well done, team," said Ms Gil. "That was a great match!"

Picture dictionary

Listen and repeat

football

match

player

score a goal

team

win

1 Look and order the story

2 Listen and say

Collins

Published by Collins
An imprint of HarperCollins*Publishers*
Westerhill Road
Bishopbriggs
Glasgow
G64 2QT

HarperCollins*Publishers*
1st Floor, Watermarque Building
Ringsend Road
Dublin 4
Ireland

William Collins' dream of knowledge for all began with the publication of his first book in 1819.

A self-educated mill worker, he not only enriched millions of lives, but also founded a flourishing publishing house. Today, staying true to this spirit, Collins books are packed with inspiration, innovation and practical expertise. They place you at the centre of a world of possibility and give you exactly what you need to explore it.

© HarperCollins*Publishers* Limited 2020

10 9 8 7 6 5 4 3 2

ISBN 978-0-00-839659-6

Collins® and COBUILD® are registered trademarks of HarperCollins*Publishers* Limited

www.collins.co.uk/elt

British Library Cataloguing in Publication Data

A catalogue record for this publication is available from the British Library.

Author: Hannah Fish
Illustrator: Dusan Pavlic (Beehive)
Series editor: Rebecca Adlard
ComMsioning editor: Zoë Clarke
Publishing manager: Lisa Todd
Product managers: Jennifer Hall and Caroline Green
In-house editor: Alma Puts Keren
Project manager: Emily Hooton
Editor: Barbara MacKay
Proofreaders: Natalie Murray and Michael Lamb
Cover designer: Kevin Robbins
Typesetter: 2Hoots Publishing Services Ltd
Audio produced by id audio, London
Reading guide author: Emma Wilkinson
Production controller: Rachel Weaver
Printed and bound by: GPS Group, Slovenia

Download the audio for this book and a reading guide for parents and teachers at www.collins.co.uk/839659